CW00392823

Tiny Tales Horror, Volume 1
Spots & Other Stories

Dave Musson

Spots first appeared in *Eidolotry #3*, by Psychotoxin Press (January 2023).

Too Late first appeared in Trembling With Fear, on horrortree (17 July 2022 edition).

CONTENTS

Praise for *Tiny Tales of Terror*, Volumes 1 &2

"The stories are short in size, but pack a huge punch in the shock and fear factor, making both collections a fun, captivating read, guaranteed to leave the reader with at least one story that will stay with them long after they've finished it…Musson has zoned in everyday fears with both volumes, fears the reader may not realize even existed. His writing is brilliant. Smooth, concise and descriptive, his words perfectly capturing the world he has crafted for his reader. His stories are horrific, scary and every uncomfortable emotion in between, yet engrossing and all too unforgettable."

Belinda Brady, reviewing for THE HORROR TREE

Tiny Tales of Terror, Volume 1

SPOTS

Mid-afternoon, Happy Woodland Nursery main office

The shrill warble of the office phone was cut off mid-ring as Emma snatched it from the cradle. Her eyes were wide with panic; she could feel the nervous sweat racing down her spine and dripping from her armpits.

'Laura?' she almost yelled into the

handpiece, ignoring all the usual phone-answering protocol. 'Laura! Speak to me!'

Emma squinted, trying to hear something positive, but the only sound that came through was a strange static, like the sort that would play from a white noise machine. Only this sound was vicious, jarring, ear-splitting. Underneath that awful racket, Emma thought she could hear the panicked voices of her colleagues.

Clara rushed over to Emma's desk and mouthed 'speaker' at her. Emma nodded and pushed the button that broadcast the call to the room. Now both women could hear the horrible, fuzzy alien squall.

'Laura!' Emma tried again. 'Laura! Matt! Kirsty! Margot!' Her hysteria inched up with each name.

Clara put a hand on Emma's arm to try and comfort her.

'Someone! Anyone, please answer!' Emma shouted.

In response, the static, but still with undertones of other voices. Then - quiet but unmistakable - came the sound of screaming.

'What was that?' Clara asked, fear etched onto her face. At the same time, there was a loud noise in their office - a *clunk,* as their door locked on its own.

Clara rushed to the door and rattled the handle, but it was no good - it had somehow been locked from the outside. She rushed back to Emma and soon both women were yelling the names of their colleagues over and over into the speaker phone, desperate for someone to pick up.

Finally, someone did. There was a heavy thud followed by a rustle as someone clumsily picked up the other end of the line.

'Laura?' Emma asked. 'Laura, is that you?'

It wasn't Laura.

Above the din of the white noise and the continued screaming underneath came the very loud sound of a toddler laughing

'Ha ha ha!'

The line went dead.

Emma and Clara looked at each other, both of them failing to find anything to say. Then the office was bleached out in a bright white light and very little mattered any more.

***

Three hours earlier, Happy Woodland Nursery main office

Clara darted back to the front office when the phone started to ring. She picked up the receiver, cutting off its shrill warble mid-flow.

'Happy Woodland Nursery,' she said on auto-pilot in her best customer-facing voice that came naturally after almost nineteen years running this delightful daycare, which offered daycare services for equally delightful middle class kids in the obviously delightful middle class haven of Kingsworth. 'Clara speaking.'

'Hey Clara, it's Laura,' the voice on the other end of the line replied.

'Hello Laura, love,' Clara said to her colleague, smiling as she did. 'Is everything OK?'

There was a brief pause as the sound of

a toddler screaming with sheer delight ran through the background before Laura spoke again with a mild chuckle.

'Can you send Emma over to the Badger Sett? Something weird is going on with the kids and we're a bit stumped by it.'

The Badger Sett was the delightfully cutesy name for the room holding the nursery's second-oldest kids - those who would turn three over the course of that academic year - and Laura was its leader. They were a fun group, old enough to actually do interesting stuff - painting, playing games with something resembling rules and structure and, as had just been evidenced, tanking around with absolute glee. The Badgers were full of beans, sure, but also still young enough to need a nap once a day, giving the staff in there a blessed hour of quiet to grab a cup of tea and let their ears recover a little. That was how it was sold to them anyway - the reality was sixty minutes or so of cleaning, tidying, and paperwork.

Clara frowned. 'Of course, Laura. What

can I tell her about it?'

Laura made a slight clicking sound, then answered.

'Spots. Two spots have appeared on the face of every child in the room today. Only they don't look like zits or anything, they're just little red circles—perfect red circles. They're on slightly different parts of their faces, but they definitely all have them.'

She paused.

'There's none of these spots on their bodies, their temperatures are all fine, and they otherwise seem totally normal. But...'

Clara waited for Laura to continue, drawing on her years of experience to know when to stay quiet and let the other person get it all out.

'Well, we'd just like another pair of eyes on them,' she finished.

'No problem Laura. I'll send Emma over now. And thanks for calling - you did the right thing.'

She replaced the phone and headed back to the kitchen to fill her business partner in on the news.

A few minutes later, Emma was heading across to the Badger Sett. She was always the one to get involved with the kids and go out to any of their four rooms if needed. It's why she and Clara were such a good team; Emma hit the front line, while Clara did all the boring financial and administrative stuff. They were each happy with their lot and, as a result, worked well together.

Emma let out a gasp as a stab of chilly November air whipped around her exposed throat, its icy fingers clawing at her neckline, desperate to be invited in. She zipped her jacket all the way up to her chin, batting away nature's chilly roaming hands.

The Badger Sett was the farthest room from the office, which meant Emma got to the full range of Happy Woodland kids on the walk over. Well, almost. The tiny ones in the baby room wouldn't be outside on a cold day like this, but all the other rooms were letting their residents enjoy some fresh air. That was part of the delightful appeal of this delightful place - outdoor experiences at every opportunity!

Emma passed the Bunny Burrow first, the room that catered to kids too old for the baby room but not ready to become a Badger yet. It was always a hilarious sight - a mixture of walking abilities that had almost two dozen little people staggering and flailing around their astroturfed garden like they were the world's youngest stag and hen parties out on a big session. Emma laughed and waved as she went past. Some children smiled at her; some looked confused. Most were too busy in their own worlds to even notice.

The vicious November wind licked at Emma's cheeks and stung her nostrils as she rounded the corner of the Bunny Burrow and moved towards the preschoolers. How those little bodies could enjoy being outside when it was this cold, she would never know. Nineteen years of working with kids hadn't explained this resistance to winter to her, and she thought not even another nineteen would either.

The preschoolers were all much more

aware of Emma as she passed their garden, and all seemed to have something Very Important to show her. She said she had to go to the Badger Sett first but promised to stop off on her way back. Being the delightful little middle-class kids they were, they all accepted Emma's answer and went back to playing.

Picking up her speed, Emma continued towards the Badger Sett, another jolt of cold wind causing her eyes to water. *Wish I'd put my hat on*, she thought as she finally made it to the little black-and-white gate.

Apart from feeling the cold, there had been nothing on Emma's walk over from the office to give her cause for concern. It was just another normal day full of normal things at the Happy Woodland Nursery. As she walked through the Badger Sett gate, closing it carefully behind her, she hoped it would stay that way.

***

Late morning, the Badger Sett Garden

A few minutes later, Emma was just as perplexed as Laura had sounded on the phone.

Every child in the Badger Sett had two little spots somewhere on their face. Some were on foreheads, some on cheeks, some on throats, but only ever two on each child.

And, just as Laura had said, they didn't look like regular spots. When Emma got close, she could see they were all actually perfectly circular - like tiny stamps - and they seemed to give off a slight but noticeable wave of heat, although they hadn't caused the children to have a fever.

'Talk me through when you noticed them,' Emma said. 'I really don't think I've ever seen anything like it.'

'I know, right?" said Laura. 'I'm glad it's not just me who thought they were weird.'

Emma grinned as the children ran in all directions across the room, avoiding clattering into her and Laura's legs as if by some unconscious obstacle-sensing safety system. Zoom! Whiz! Whoosh! Just as in all the other gardens for all the other rooms, everything seemed normal here. The kids were busy living their best, delightful lives. To Emma's left, a small gang appeared to be Going On A Bear Hunt; to her right, a trio used toy cars as paintbrushes on a large sheet of paper. On the far side of the garden, the mud kitchen was proving as popular as ever, while coming towards them were two boys, each holding a piece of string and giggling hysterically. Attached to the pieces of string were small tree branches.

Emma raised her eyebrow, and Laura turned to follow her gaze. She laughed.

'Ah, dog logs. We played that game in Forest School on Monday and those two have been obsessed ever since!'

'Very cute,' Emma said.

'Sorry, the spots,' said Laura. 'Well, I noticed them first on Archie.'

'Archie Hopkinson?' asked Emma, almost without thinking.

'No, Archie Andrews,' Laura replied, also without thought - the running joke of

11

the two Archies had simply become part of the Happy Woodland vernacular, 'although I did find them on Archie Hopkinson later. Anyway, not long after I saw them, Matt found some on Sammie, Lola, and Lily; Kirsty saw them on Aubrey and Zach; and then Margot found some on George, Millie, and Joseph. That's everyone who's in today.'

'Strange,' said Emma, barely aware she'd spoken the word out loud.

'Really strange,' Laura agreed, 'but, as I said to Clara, none of the kids have a fever. All their nappies and toilet doings are normal and, as you can see, they're as lively as ever.'

Laura flung her arms out to indicate the normal maelstrom of Badger Sett fun that was going on around them. Unfortunately, it was right at the same time that one of the dog log-toting children was walking past. Laura's hand caught him across the side of the head, which was covered in a delightful, hand-knitted rainbow woolly hat, and the little chap flopped to the leaf-covered ground.

'Oh, Aubrey!' Laura turned bright red. 'I'm so sorry! Let me help you up.'

It was only then Emma realised how quiet the garden had become. Seconds ago, the air had been filled with the sound of toddlers having a great time. But now, nothing. It was as close to silent as being outside could get - and not just here in the Badger Sett Garden. It seemed as though every child on the premises had been muted.

The fallen child – Aubrey - was trying to get onto his hands and knees, adding a fresh layer of mud to his already-filthy jumpsuit in the process. Emma also bent towards him to help set him back on his feet, but not before glancing to her side.

They were being watched. The children had all stopped and were staring at Laura and her. The eyes of every child in the Badger Sett Garden were on her and, even though she couldn't see them, she knew all of the other children on site right now were doing the same.

Emma saw this, but didn't really take it in, as her instinct was still to help pick

Aubrey up. Only once he was back on his feet and holding the string attached to his dog log did Emma realise the eeriness of that scene.

She snapped her head up and looked around.

No one was looking at her. The garden was as it always was: full of life, with the volume cranked accordingly. The mud kitchen, the Bear Hunt, the painting cars…they were all in full swing. None of the other staff had seemed to notice what she had.

Laura stood up and dusted her hands on her trousers as Aubrey and his pal continued on their dog log walk.

'I really should have learned to not talk with my arms by now!' she said.

Both women laughed.

'What do you think, then, about these spots?'

'They're weird, but I don't think they're dangerous. Just make sure you tell every parent about them at pick up later, explain that they're otherwise fine, and ask them to keep an eye on them.'

'OK.' Laura smiled. 'Thanks for coming out in the cold to see us. I feel like I've wasted your time a bit.'

Emma shook her head. 'Not at all. That's what I'm here for. You did the right thing. Call me if anything changes.'

'Will do. Thanks again, Emma.'

Laura jogged after Aubrey, obviously still feeling awful about knocking the little guy over despite him having long-since moved on. Emma took one final look around the garden. She still felt like she was being watched, but as her eyes struggled to keep up with everything that was going on in front, she told herself she was being silly—that she'd imagined what had happened a few moments earlier.

And she probably *had* been watched. Any time a Grown Up From The Office came outside, it was a big event—a spectator sport, in fact—and the kids would usually gawp at the strange-but-familiar visitor.

She left the Badger Sett Garden and headed back to the office, not forgetting to stop in with the preschoolers and to see all of those Very Important Things they had to share with her. And they were, indeed, Very Important…depending on your definition of important of course.

***

Nothing of note happened for the next hour and a half.

***

Mid-afternoon, Happy Woodland Nursery main office

This time, it was Emma who answered the office phone.

'Happy Woodland Nursery,' she said. 'Emma speaking.'

'Hi, Emma. It's Matt, over in the Badger Sett,' said the voice at the other end. 'Laura asked me to give you an update on the spots situation.'

'Oh, yes. What's going on with them?'

'Well, the spots are all still there, but everything else is fine. No fevers, no unusual behaviour. Nothing weird.'

'Did lunch go OK?' asked Emma.

'Yep. They had cheesy pasta - popular as ever! In fact…' he paused.

'Go on, Matt,' Emma said.

'Well, that was something slightly different,' he continued. 'I've never seen them so hungry, every single one of them. They were ravenous - we actually ran out of food!'

Emma let out a small laugh. 'Oh wow. Bet that was unpopular.'

'Now you mention it, they did all go quiet when I explained they'd eaten everything. They all stared at me at the same time, like they were genuinely angry with me.'

Emma's stomach was suddenly full of butterflies. Her face lost some of its colour and she became aware of her heartbeat in her ears. She was instantly back in the garden that morning, feeling the combined burning gaze of every child on site.

'At least, it felt like that.' Matt's voice snapped Emma back to the present. 'But I probably imagined it. It's just that they usually *never* stop talking when they're round the table.'

Emma felt the knot in her core slowly unravel and she let out the breath she didn't know she was holding.

'Anyway, that's all I have to add. Margot and Kirsty are just getting the last few down for their naps.'

'OK. Thanks for the update, Matt. If you can have someone from the room check in towards the end of the day with another, that would be really helpful. Have a fun afternoon.'

It was only after she'd hung up that Emma noticed the dark - almost black - spiral she'd carved into her notebook with a pencil she didn't realise she'd been holding. Round and round and round until, at some point unknown to her, the stick of graphite had snapped - actually snapped - in half. There were splinters in Emma's palm and even a few drops of blood, but she hadn't even felt it.

Why am I so worried? she thought. *Everything is fine, so why have I snapped a pencil in half?*

Emma stared at the broken writing implement and the doom-filled black spiral she'd scrawled for a moment, then shook her head. It was fine. Everything was fine.

She took herself off to the kitchen to microwave her can of tomato soup.

***

Naptime, Badger Sett room

As Matt replaced the phone in its cradle, Kirsty and Margot tidied the line debris left abandoned by the now-sleeping toddlers in the corner of the room. Cuddly toys, model cars, wooden kitchen utensils, even a rogue glove - it was like a two-year-old had taken over an episode of *The Generation Game*, or at least been given the task of choosing that week's prizes

While Kirsty carried an armful of crap over to the toy box, Margot bent over to pick up a book. As she did, she caught a reflection of something strange in the plastic storage boxes mounted to the wall out of the corner of her eye.

It looked as though all of the children were sitting bolt upright, staring at her.

She half-jumped and quickly looked away from the reflection towards the kids.

They were asleep. All of them.

Margot shook her head and grabbed the book, only to subsequently drop the three *Hey Duggee* figures she was holding in her other hand.

Sighing, she scrabbled over to grab them from where they'd landed near the full-length mirror the team had installed so the children could enjoy pulling faces at themselves. Margot glanced in the mirror and properly jumped this time.

Again, the children were all sat bolt upright, staring at her with looks of pure hatred and fury.

Trying to keep her breathing steady, she slowly turned back to the room. No children staring at her. They were all still sleeping. Was she imagining it?

Margot dumped the toys in their box and hurried back to the rest of the staff, still holding the discarded book.

Kirsty, Matt, and Laura were making

cups of tea when they saw Margot's expression. All of them felt their pulse quicken.

'What's wrong, Margot?' asked Laura.

Before she could answer, things started happening.

The drawers in the small kitchen area of the Badger Sett flew open, then slammed shut one at a time, while the kids' coats and bags rattled so hard on their colourful pegs that they spilled onto the floor.

'What on earth—' began Kirsty, when the two doors to the Sett - the main entrance and the emergency exit - locked from the inside with a defiant and definite *click*.

The staff looked at each other, then turned to the nap area to check on the children.

They were no longer asleep.

Every child's eyes were open, and they were slowly getting to their feet. First Sammie, then Lola, then Lily. Next was Aubrey. Archie Andrews and Archie Hopkinson stood up together, Zach following immediately after.

George, Millie, and Josh did the same behind this group, but they were blocked from view. None of the children smiled, none of them talked; none of them even blinked.

Once they were all on their feet, they started walking towards the staff. As they did, they linked hands, forming a circle around the adults, still looking like they were in some shared sleepwalking fever dream.

Just as Laura was about to say something to the children, they all formed a perfect *O* shape with their mouths. Then, the singing started. Only it wasn't singing, not really.

It was *broadcasting*.

'Ring-a-ring-a-roses,' the children chanted and started to skip around the adults in perfect time with each other, with the kind of grace and balance normal two-year-olds don't possess, 'a pocketful of posies. Atishoo, atishoo, we all … fall …'

The children stopped skipping.

'… downnnnnnnnnnnnnnnnnnnnn,' they

finished, holding the final note for an unnaturally long time.

Rather than cut the sound off, that final consonant seemed to break up, like a radio losing signal, morphing into white noise - loud, ear-splitting white noise.

The adults instinctively huddled closer to each other for protection from the circle of hissing toddlers. The children took a step towards them, still making that awful sound.

Another step. Laura noticed that one of the Archies was holding the phone, but she was too terrified to even work out which Archie it was.

The children took another step together and, as they did, their eyes all started glowing a hideous, toxic bright yellow.

They took another step towards the adults and the volume of the white noise coming from their mouths ramped up several notches. That's when the grown-ups started to scream. They looked around in a blind panic for a way out, but there was none. The circle was complete, the children coming closer - each with their mouths open, their eyes glowing, and two small, perfectly circular spots somewhere on their face, now more prominent than they'd been all day.

The spots looked alive.

Kirsty noticed Archie holding the phone - Archie Hopkinson, as it happened - laughing into it, before pushing the big red button to cut off whoever was on the other line. She felt scared adult hands grabbing hers and pressed herself against the rest of her colleagues in the middle of the awful circle.

The white noise was excruciating, the adults screaming themselves hoarse and then, the room bleached out in a bright, white light.

All the noise, all the horror, was lost in the glow.

***

Home time, Happy Woodland Nursery car park

Paul yanked the strap on his son's car seat tight, securing him in place, and then swivelled him round to face the iPad that was mounted to the back of the passenger seat. The current hit video - that one of some Japanese guy pushing *Thomas the Tank Engine* toys down a ramp into a bucket of mud - was already playing and Aubrey locked onto it straight away.

'Let's go home, dude,' Paul said, then shut the car door. As he walked around the back of the vehicle, dropping his son's nursery bag in the boot and then continuing round to the driver's door, he found himself chewing over the weirdness that had been tonight's pick-up.

First, Aubrey seemed quieter than usual. Then again, it was a Friday - a Friday after a long week - and today's good weather would have undoubtedly been maximised by the nursery staff, with as much time spent running the garden as possible. *Probably just tired*, Paul thought.

Second, the staff appeared off-kilter too. Not just tired, but almost coming in and out of focus. Even during the course of the two-minute handover chat, Matt had seemed to lose the thread a couple of times - and Kirsty did the same with Archie Andrews' parents, from what Paul had overheard.

Still, he thought, *toddlers are exhausting. That's the big secret everyone keeps from you before you become a parent: how you come to dread weekends and how going back to work on a Monday is actually a chance to relax and recharge. They're probably just shattered, like I will be by Sunday afternoon.*

Paul pushed his key into the ignition and started the car. He flipped on the headlights to cut through the dark November afternoon and plugged his iPod back into the USB hub. That was the deal he'd struck with Aubrey for car journeys - videos in the back for the little dude, Daddy's music up front for Paul, so long as he didn't turn it up too loud. And yes, Paul still had an iPod. Streaming be damned, he liked owning his music, even if it was still digital.

The opening riff of *Swarm* by Palm Reader whirled around Paul as he pulled out of the car park, his mind still ticking over.

It was the weird conversation about the spots that sat the most uncomfortably with him.

Paul wasn't too concerned about the spots themselves; sure, he'd never seen such perfect circles on his son's face before, but Matt had assured him that Aubrey didn't have a fever and that, apart from those little dots, was his normal self. Paul had tried some cliché dad quip in response to this - *Uh-oh, still a cheeky monkey, then!* -but it coincided with one of those strange lapses from Matt, where he seemed to check out for a moment.

What was bugging Paul the most was how every child was now heading home with a pair of spots somewhere on their face. The nursery staff were clearly having the same conversation with all the parents, and it was probably nothing, but all the other kids Paul had seen at pick-up had the same subdued vibe that his own did.

And, now he thought of it, hadn't Paul noticed two perfectly circular spots on

Matt's face as they were talking? And on Kirsty's too?

Forget it, Paul thought as he signalled left and made the most of a gap in traffic by joining the main road and easing all the way up to fifth gear. *They're all just tired. It's that time of year - Christmas is in sight, but still a few weeks left to get through before we get a break.*

They're just tired, he thought again as *Swarm* gave way to the hypnotic, lumbering riff of *Internal Winter* that always calmed Paul right down.

In the back seat, Aubrey was staring at the video on the mounted iPad, but he wasn't watching it.

He was perfectly still, waiting. Then, as if responding to some silent cue, his mouth dropped into a perfect *O* and he started to make a strange crackling sound, like white noise.

The sound from Aubrey's mouth grew louder, loud enough to seep into Paul's music. Paul frowned at the interference and tried jiggling the cable that connected his iPod to the car stereo, while also keeping his eyes on the road ahead.

As the noise got louder, Aubrey's eyes started glowing bright yellow. They reflected off the slightly-tilted iPad screen and onto the ceiling of the car - two throbbing yellow spots.

The car cruised towards a crossroads and, as it did, Aubrey turned his glowing gaze towards his father.

TOO LATE

Finally, the light on Paul's new printer turned blue and it made a pleasant *ding!* noise.

'Aha!' said Paul, grinning, 'got it!'

He walked to the bottom of the stairs and shouted up, 'Dylan!'

A few seconds later, his seven-year-old appeared, that beautiful, kind, and hilarious kid that had somehow been the product of Paul's loins and nurturing.

'Yes Daddy?' Dylan said.

'I've finally got the printer working - can you try sending something to print out for me please? You should be able to connect to it from the Wifi.'

Dylan smiled.

'Ooh yes!' he said, and darted back into his room.

Paul heard the sounds of fingers hitting a keyboard, then a few clicks of a mouse, before the sounds shifted back to his study, as the printer whirred into life and started to *chug, chug, chug* as it made whatever was on Dylan's screen right now appear on paper.

The printer gave a final flourish and another pleasant noise - this one almost like a satisfied sigh of a job well done - before going quiet. Paul went over to it, picked up the sheet of paper it had spat out, and read it.

HELLO DADDY :-) was printed in bright blue letters.

Paul started to chuckle.

Dylan came tanking down the stairs, full of beans.

'Did it work Daddy?' he asked as he ran into the room.

Paul simply held up the sheet and showed his son. Dylan started to laugh, and Paul followed. It was good laughter, it was real laughter, it was the kind of laughter you'd like to bottle up and keep forever.

***

The next day, Dylan was at school and Paul was sat working in his study like usual and, like usual, was in deep concentration - ploughing through this month's sales report. When he was in that zone - when he practically fell into the screen and became one with the numbers and charts found there - very little could shake his attention. He was so familiar with the sounds of his study and the daytime quiet of the house that only a new noise would break through.

A noise like his new printer, which announced itself to Paul with that pleasant *ding!* from yesterday.

Paul looked up and frowned and the machine started that *chug, chug, chug* of printing. A few moments later, it spat out a sheet and sighed its satisfied sigh.

Paul reached over and looked at the sheet.

HELLO DADDY :-(it said, in bright blue letters. Paul started to smile, thinking that somehow Dylan had triggered the thing to send something to print as a midafternoon surprise for his old man, when he spotted something that stopped the smile midflow.

The smiley…it was no longer smiling. It was showing the unhappy version.

'What the?' Paul asked the room, when the printer started whirring again - *chug, chug, chug* until and final spit and sigh.

DADDY this second sheet said, but already a third was following. *Chug, chug, chug* - the noises growing louder, and louder, and more intense, and more oppressive in Paul's head.

HELP the third sheet said and Paul's blood went cold.

'This must be a joke,' Paul muttered,

trying to convince himself of something he knew wasn't true, but ran upstairs anyway to check Dylan's laptop.

The laptop was shut, of course, and Paul darted back downstairs, coming back into his study just in time to hear the printer sigh again. He looked down, and saw a small pile of papers, which he picked up with trembling hands.

DADDY the first sheet said, then THE MAN, then THE MAN IN THE PIG MASK, then HE'S TAKEN ME, then SORRY, and finally HELP ME - all in that same cheery blue, which now looked a lot less wholesome.

His heart pounding, Paul fumbled for his phone and dialled his son's number. It went straight to voicemail.

'Dylan, it's Daddy,' Paul said, trying to sound as calm as possible, 'This is going to sound very silly, but I've just had a weird feeling about you and want to know you're ok. I'm sure you're on the bus home and your phone is in your bag which is why you didn't answer, but just call me as soon as you hear this, ok? Nothing to worry about, just your old dad having a wobble. Anyway, just ring me - love you Dylan.'

In a moment of sheer horror, the second he disconnected the call, the printer started up again - *chug, chug, chug*, then a spit and sigh.

One word this time, and a different colour too; NO, it said, in blood red.

Paul reached for his phone again, planning to call Dylan, Dylan's best friend Nate, the school...anyone, when that awful *chug, chug, chug* of the printer started again.

Rooted to the spot, Paul felt the dread take over as he watched that final sheet of paper fly out of the printer with such force that it floated right off the desk and onto the floor. Suddenly aware of a terrible whooshing in his ears, Paul bent down, picked up the paper, and turned it over.

TOO LATE the blood-red letters said, and Paul dropped the paper like it was too hot to touch.

The printer sighed its satisfied sigh, flashed red three times, then switched itself off.

WHERE'S BRUCE?

Jacob's heart sank when he saw that book back on his shelf. How was it even possible? He'd watched Daddy burn the thing the other night.

And yet, there it was - nestled between *The Very Hungry Caterpillar* and *The Tiger Who Came to Tea* - the friendly blue letters on the spine giving no indication of the horrors within.

Where's Bruce? by Regina Farraday.

Jacob might only have been four years old, but he still knew evil when it landed in his lap and that book had scared him from the moment he first saw it. His Daddy had come round to agreeing with him eventually, but only after the bad things happened.

Where's Bruce? had been given to Jacob by his clueless aunt last Christmas. She'd clearly just seen the big, friendly, black and white-spotted dog on the front cover, noted it was a lift-the-flap book - Jacob's favourite type - and so had bought it, wrapped it, and posted it. She wasn't to blame - part of the book's evil was looking innocent.

In fact, most adults flicking through *Where's Bruce?* wouldn't see a thing wrong with it - each double page had a series of flaps where, under one, Bruce the dalmatian would be hiding. It was cute, it was fun.

It was awful.

The horror lay in the background of each scene. Subtle things wrong with the illustration that a 'grown-up' mind would gladly ignore.

Jacob saw them, though, and knew they were bad. It was only when they started to happen in real life that he got scared.

First of all, it was almost funny; the dropped birthday cake on page 2 mirroring what happened to Jacob's sister Eve that January, or the cat with the bandaged paw on page 4 - just like their family moggie Peach would need after she mistimed her jump from the kitchen worktop a few weeks ago and ended up on a different work surface - the vet's.

But, they soon stopped being funny. The confused-looking old woman on page 8 whose face matched that of Jacob's granny on the day Daddy told him how she had *themensha* and had to move into a home, that was creepy.

However, when the little girl - who looked just like Eve - suddenly disappeared on page 11, having previously been on every spread Jacob instantly felt sick the moment he noticed it. When his sister vanished that afternoon, he couldn't help but feel guilty.

It was only when he showed Daddy the background of page 19 - the sleeping woman surrounded by what Jacob had thought were M&Ms who looked just like Mummy did when they discovered her overdose - *that* was when an adult finally believed him.

That was two days ago, and Daddy had burned the book in front of his eyes. They'd even spread the ashes in four different places around town.

And yet, here it was, back on Jacob's shelf - he had to get Daddy. But, before he did that, he pulled it from his bookcase with trembling arms and flicked through the pages.

The images inside were different now. No weird background happenings, instead, every spread was Bruce the dalmatian. At a glance he still looked like a big, happy, friendly dog. Until you saw how crazy his eyes looked.

And, under every flap was a little boy and his Daddy hiding in fear.

Jacob gasped and shouted for his Daddy, who came running. As they looked at the book together and tried to come up with a plan, they heard something from outside the front door.

The sound of a dog growling.

Tiny Tales of Terror, Volume 1

NIGHTTIME ROUTINE

Each night before bed, she goes round every single door and window in her house and checks them.

She tests every handle - every one - ensuring they're locked with a quick jiggle. For the back door, she often unlocks it just to re-lock it again and be totally certain it is done.

She does the downstairs ones first, then upstairs. Then, she comes back downstairs and checks them all again. Every single night, the same routine, the same set of stringent tests.

I know this because I'm there too - every night, hiding at the bottom of her garden, watching, and waiting. One day, she's going to miss something - I'm certain of it. And, when she does, that's when I'll let myself in.

DARK

It wasn't just dark; it was pitch black.

'I wasn't expecting black-out blinds to make this much difference,' said Windy.

'I know,' said Sam from the other side of the bed, which - without the visual cues - could either have been six inches or six feet away, 'I don't think I've ever been in a bedroom this dark before.'

They both lay there for a moment in silence.

'Did I ever tell you that the dark kind of freaks me out?' said Windy, her voice dropping to a whisper without her even realising.

'Shall I put a light on?' said Sam, also in a whisper.

'No, no,' said Windy, 'I'll cope.'

More silence.

Windy suddenly sat up, pointlessly squinting into the darkness.

'What's up?' said Sam.

'I thought I heard something,' Windy replied, 'from the corner of the room.'

Sam flicked the bedside light on, and the room's previous blackness was pushed back by a glow of warm light. There was nothing in the room that shouldn't have been there.

'I can leave this on if you like?' said Sam, looking up at Windy.

'No, don't be silly,' she said, 'once I get to sleep I'll be fine. Turn the light back off. The whole point of getting those blinds was to help us sleep better - it'll be good for us.'

Sam did. Just as the darkness engulfed

the room again Windy thought she saw the shape of a tall person in the corner of the room, but she did her best to ignore it. She lay down and shut her eyes.

'We can always get a night light, you know?' whispered Sam, 'I have to say, the room being this dark is even giving me the creeps a bit.'

'We can't get a night light!' giggled Windy quietly, 'surely not?'

That got them both laughing, loud enough to block out the creak of a floorboard near that corner of the room where Windy's stressed brain had tricked her into seeing a figure.

A few minutes later, Sam and Windy were both breathing deeply, sound asleep. The figure of the night watched them both, crawling onto the ceiling to get a better view. Tonight wasn't the night to reveal himself to them - he'd stay dark a bit longer yet, let them get used to their pitch black room and stop creeping themselves out.

Only then would he let himself be seen. It was *far* more fun that way.

Tiny Tales of Terror, Volume 1

UNEXPECTED

As she staggered through the deserted junkyard, frantically trying to find somewhere to hide or something she could use to kill that damned doll, June had a revelation.

This is not what I thought being a housewife would be like, she thought.

She glanced over her shoulder to see if the doll was still following her and, yes, of course it was. Whatever had possessed that hideous thing meant to see June dead. Its garish orange hair stood out against the dirty grey piles of junk.

The thing smiled and carried on shuffling towards June.

It was hard to believe that, just two weeks ago, June was still working for the agency - even if she was counting down the days to marrying Herb and giving it all up. He earned more than enough, and she had plans to volunteer at lots of local charities.

The doll was a downright weird wedding present from Herb's Great Aunt - who the fuck gives a *doll* as a wedding parent to two, fully grown adults anyway? - and June had hated it from the start; its pink gingham dress clashed horribly with that tangerine hair, and the things dead eyes gave her the creeps.

It had only taken a few days for June to realise something was wrong with that doll. It kept appearing in rooms it shouldn't, and there didn't seem to be a day go by where June didn't catch a flash of pink or orange streaking through her peripheral vision.

Just stress, June had thought initially, *it's all the stress from the wedding flooding out of me now we're all done.*

But it wasn't. Deep down June had always known it, and when she got home from the supermarket earlier to find Herb's bloody body on the kitchen floor with the doll still stabbing him relentlessly, it all made sense.

Running to the junkyard hadn't been a conscious decision - June had opted for flight instead of fight and her legs had taken over.

She heard a clang of something scarily close behind her and realised she needed to hurry up and end this. To her left was a discarded baseball bat held together with gaffa tape, which might work temporarily, but she understood that - ultimately - she needed something sharp, something that could cut and tear.

Still, she grabbed the bat - better that than nothing at all.

June looked up and saw what looked like various pieces of old kitchens and decided that would be where she might find something. She put on another burst of pace.

The doll giggled and kept closing in.

If I get out of this, June thought between deep breaths, *I'm going to kill Herb's aunt.*

June fled across the junkyard, and the possessed doll followed.

BAD DREAM

Just as he was about to see what horrendous damage had been done to his screaming son's delicate face, Vlad woke with a gasp.

What a fucking horrible dream.

He gently rolled over and stared at the baby monitor, which sat in its cradle on Vlad's bedside table. Nothing. No screaming, no crying, just the usual gentle hum of the white noise machine. In other words, just a normal night.

Vlad sighed and rolled onto his back. His heart was still pounding from those awful images his brain had dreamt up, so there was no point in trying to get back to sleep for the time being.

Instead, he looked up at the black bedroom ceiling and tried to calm down. He focused on the slow, steady breathing of his wife who was sound asleep next to him, and tried to match his breathing with hers.

It helped. It soothed. But he was still too wired to go back to sleep - something he accepted willingly and, the moment he did, his shoulders relaxed and he was able to take stock.

Feeling better, Vlad went over that terrible dream in his head again. It was bizarre, weird, and downright disturbing.

For one, he hadn't been at home. He'd been at his parents' house - the house where Vlad had grown up - and, for some reason, was out running on the street. As he passed the house, he heard the unmistakable sound of his young son crying - no, *screaming* - from inside.

In the dream, he opened the front door, and popped his head into the lounge. There was no-one there. For whatever reason, his parents had left their only grandchild alone in their house.

The Vlad in the dream felt angry, but had no real time to worry about it as his son was still howling upstairs. Vlad climbed them, heading to the back of the house - his childhood room - pissed off at his parents but desperately wanting to reach his son and soothe him.

As dream Vlad entered his old bedroom, he saw his son in a cot placed under the window. He was huddled up in the far corner, face pressed into the join of the wooden panels and looking away from Vlad. He was still screaming too, and it broke Vlad's heart.

Dream Vlad's mood quickly changed, though, when he approached the cot. He saw something scuttle away from his son towards the opposite side of the cot. It looked like a pillowcase, only one the size of an envelope.

A pillowcase with a thin tail sticking out of it.

With mounting horror, Vlad bent over the cot and grabbed the small cloth package. The moment he did, whatever was inside squirmed and squeaked.

Vlad braced himself, then pulled the edge of the material back to reveal the face of the rat he knew he was going to see. It was vile and its teeth and snout were dripping with blood - Vlad's son's blood.

Without thinking, Vlad quickly opened the bedroom window and threw the pillowcase - and the rat sitting in it - outside. However, it didn't travel anywhere near as far as it should have done; the rat landed on the roof of the conservatory that sat under the bedroom, and immediately began sprinting back to the open window, its now red eyes glaring at Vlad.

Vlad was just able to slam the window shut in time before the rat ran into it, scratching manically to be let in.

Then came the dream's scariest part. Moving in slow motion, Vlad turned to the corner of the cot. He lowered shaking hands into the corner, held his son's body, and turned him over to see what the rat had done.

And that's when he woke up.

Reliving it now, safe in the knowledge it was all a dream, was no better. Vlad rolled back into his usual sleeping position and tried to close his eyes, but every time he did he was back in that room about to see his son's face.

The only way he'd be able to get back to sleep would be to look at his son - in the real world - and put his mind at ease.

Vlad rolled off the mattress and edged his way around the bed frame, successfully avoiding the toe-stubbing hazards of both the bed frame and the edge of the cupboards that lined two walls of the room. He gently opened the bedroom door.

His bare feet padded on the landing carpet and he walked towards his son's room and turned the door handle.

Immediately, something felt wrong.

Vlad had assumed this task would be mainly administrative - go into his son's room, see his still undamaged and beautiful face, tuck him back in and then go back to bed himself. So why was Vlad's heart thumping again then?

First to hit Vlad was the smell - pennies. That unmistakable coppery smell of spilled blood. Then, the noises. Hidden just under the rumble of the white noise was a pattering - a scuttering.

No, Vlad thought, and rushed towards the cot where his son lay in what looked like a sleeping position.

Even in the dark, Vlad could tell the tiny mattress was blood soaked. Something awful darted into the corner of the cot away from his son, no mini pillowcase this time, but Vlad barely even noticed it - all his focus was on the tiny bundle in a sleeping bag.

His son.

Vlad lowered shaking hands into the corner, held his son's body, and turned him over to see what the rat - the real world rat - had done.

This time, Vlad didn't wake up. This time, he got to see the story all the way to the end.

Tiny Tales of Terror, Volume 1

FACE IN THE CROWD

He stood at the window of his penthouse apartment, whisky in hand, and stared down at the masses below. The peasants.

The plebs.

As always, they were toiling; fighting for space, for water, for any sort of hope of getting things back to what they were. Little did they know the man who'd caused all this misery was not only a few metres above them, but that he spent all day watching them suffer, like a spectator sport.

Back in that apartment, he sipped his whisky and felt no remorse. The decisions he'd been made were ones he'd make again in a heartbeat. He didn't care a bit for the greater good, he cared about himself and himself only.

Scanning over the crowd of helpless wasters, he smirked to himself. Wherever he looked, there was suffering, and it made him feel special to know he'd caused it.

To his left, a filthy woman cradling what looked like a dead baby in her arms as she wept, wept, wept.

To his right, two men were in a knife fight over a crust of stale, mouldy bread. Stabbing, thrusting, *cutting*.

And, directly below him, a figure with a boar's head was looking right back at him.

The man did a double take.

Yep, there was a person with a boar's head looking right at him. Not moving, not doing anything - just staring.

From up here in his lap of luxury, the

man couldn't tell if this person actually had a boar's head or if it was just a mask. It had to be a mask, right?

The man downed the rest of his whisky, not taking his eyes off the boar person. The boar person stared right back, slowly chilling the man with each second.

Finally, the man pulled his gaze away and looked off to the right. There was another boar person, also looking back at him.

This wasn't fun any more. The man's eyes started to dart around the crowd and, everywhere they landed, he saw another boar person. Within seconds there seemed to be hundreds of them, all staring at him.

Suddenly, the man heard a low scream and realised all the boar people were pointing up at him. When they did, the masses all stopped what they were doing and looked up too. The man was frozen with fear - they all saw him, and knew him for what he was.

Then, just as quickly as it had started, the scream cut out. The masses, and the boar people, dropped their gaze. The man breathed a sigh of relief.

And that's when they charged towards the entrance to his building. It was time for some payback.

UNDERNEATH

Marcy woke with a jolt and was instantly grateful for the night light - even if she had teased Maisy about it.

The gentle, blue-tinged glow of that light was surprisingly calming, and Marcy's heart slowed to a more normal speed. She took a moment just to stare at the ceiling and listen to the soft snores of her sister from across the room.

She'd had nightmares before of course

- what kid with even a moderately active imagination hadn't? - but most of them would fade quickly as soon as she woke up. Not this one. This one was lingering.

Marcy actually knew where this one had come for a change - her older brother. Or, more accurately, that Stephen King book he was reading. Kieran had set it down yesterday evening to go and make a snack and, foolishly, Marcy had decided to peek at it, wanting to know what was so scary about the writing of some old American guy.

The book was *The Outsider* and it only took one line to unsettle Marcy's 10-year-old brain. One of the characters said how they'd dreamed there had been someone lying under their bed all night, looking up at them.

When Marcy had read that line, she went cold inside and inside put the book down. But, those hooks were lodged in her head and she couldn't shake them. Part of the deal of being 10 really.

When she and Maisy had gone to bed that night, Marcy had rolled out the nightly joshing of her younger sister - making fun of her for still wanting the night light - but it was half-hearted. She could still feel that line from the book caressing the back of her neck.

Naturally, the bad dream had come and it had been exactly what she'd been expecting; that there was someone lying on their back under her bed doing nothing else but staring up at her - through the wooden slats, through the mattress, through the comfy mattress topper, the sheet, and looking at her sleeping. The thing that woke her up was when the figure's hand slowly started to come out from under the bed, and moved slowly up the side towards her.

Now, though, she knew two things; it was all just a dream and she had no plans of reading any more of Kieran's books any time soon.

Marcy rolled back onto her front - her favourite sleeping position - ready to doze off again, and just happened to glance over at Maisy's side of the room before she did.

There was her younger sister, still

sound asleep with a teddy bear stuffed under her chin and one hand dangling out from the covers and over the side of the bed. Maisy smiled then glanced under her sister's bed.

Someone was there.

Just like in her dream, there was a figure under the bed and looking up at her sister. Marcy gasped. When she did, the figure turned its face towards her.

Its eyes glowed red - the polar opposite of the calming blue night light - and it flashed a smile that showed far too many teeth, all of which were sharp and pointed.

Marcy breathed in to scream but the figure pointed at her and she was instantly mute and unable to move. The figure shook its head slowly and wagged its finger. Then, it slowly moved its claw - it didn't have normal hands - out from under the bed and up towards Maisy's soft, dangling hand.

Tears streaming down her face, body locked to her mattress, Marcy screamed at the top of her voice but it was a sound that only played in her head. The figure's claw slowly closed around Maisy's wrist.

Tiny Tales of Terror, Volume 1

EYES

'I'm going to turn off the light now champ,' Reece said, 'just remember that there's nothing here trying to get you. Those things you saw that you thought were a monster's eyes are just the streetlights outside catching your teddy bear's eyes instead - there are no monsters here, ok?'

'Yes dad,' said Archie, 'love you.'

'Love you too buddy,' said Reece. He

turned off the light and closed Archie's door.

Instantly, those eyes were staring at him - red and glowing.

Archie wanted to scream for his dad, but knew he *couldn't* - knew he was being a baby and that those evil eyes were *simply not real*. They belonged to his teddy, that was all.

He closed his own eyes, counted to ten, then opened them. The red eyes had gone. It had just been his imagination.

Archie sighed and rolled over onto his side.

The red eyes were staring at him again, this time from the other side of the room. He bit the inside of his cheeks hard enough to draw blood while stifling another scream and instead screwed his eyes shut.

Again, he counted - trying for 20 this time but only making it to 19 before his mind got the better of him and pushed his eyelids open.

There was nothing staring at him, just his darkened room - those familiar things cast in shadow like his chair, his small desk, his toy chest, the shelves and photos on his walls, and his wardrobe were kind of creepy, but nothing to lose sleep over.

Archie carefully glanced back round to his original view, towards the chair by his window where those red eyes had first appeared. He saw...

Nothing. Just the chair, and his teddy bear - just like dad had said.

Archie felt a huge weight lift from his chest and thought he was *finally* ready to sleep. He cursed his own imagination for being so active - even if it had helped him win that prize in creative writing last week.

He turned back on his side, brought his legs up into a sort-of fetal position and snuggled around to get comfortable.

He opened his eyes one last time, just to glance at the digital clock next to his bed like he did most nights.

That's when he saw them.

The eyes. Red, raging, and right there on the pillow next to him. Archie didn't have time to scream. The owner of the eyes was too quick.

By the time Reece found what was left

of him the next morning, it was really quite an awful sight.

BEDTIME

Bedtime again. Storytime, again. The same story as every night, of course, and that was absolutely fine - it's the only one that did the trick.

Some days she couldn't quite believe how quickly bedtime came around again, others it felt like every second leading up to it had lasted an hour - the countdown to the 'grownup' part of an evening that followed an agonising eternity still to wade through.

Anyway, tonight's bedtime was here, which meant a story. Much as she'd love to pick one of the dozens of so-far unread books from the shelf and discover a colourful new world, there was no point in rocking the boat. This one worked. Probably because her son had the same name as the lead character.

There was once upon a time a poor widow who had an only son named Jack, and a cow named Milky-White.

Reading the same tale every single night was, obviously, frustrating as hell. But it was also part of being a parent. When it comes to sleep, if you find a formula that works you absolutely do not mess with it. She often thought this idea was the birth of that phrase about what you should do with things that aren't broke.

All they had to live on was the milk the cow gave every morning, which they carried to the market and sold - until one morning Milky-White gave no milk.

That wasn't to say that part of her mind didn't niggle away at her. Is all this repetition bad for her own Jack's development? How is he going to expand his brain if it's the same story every night? But, on the flip side, getting a solid night of shut-eye was also doing him good, right? It certainly did her good.

'What shall we do, what shall we do?' said the widow, wringing her hands.

Her friends sympathised with her - at some point they'd all been in the same situation with their own kids, where only a particular story would do. That made it a little easier to grab that familiar book with the cover she now knew every inch of and open those pages again and again.

'Cheer up mother, I'll go and get work somewhere,' said Jack.

Her mother, on the other hand, did not approve. She saw it as a sign of weakness, but she was from a completely different generation of parenting - an unsympathetic one, a generation that could not and did not deal with any type of conflict, probably because of their own lifetime of pent-up trauma that they've never come close to acknowledging, let alone dealing with. It was the same reason her mother couldn't bear it any time Jack expressed himself with the only tool he had - crying. A crying baby triggered 'Operation Distract With Lots Of Loud Cooing Noises' from her mum. With that in mind, her mother's reaction was no surprise.

'We've tried that before, and nobody would take you,' said his mother. 'We must sell Milky-White and with the money, start a shop or something.'

Anyway, what did it matter? This was *her* son after all. She knew best.

Her son. Her perfect, beautiful, dead boy.

Her child, who had never ever actually been in this house, let alone this room or this cot. Jack's entire seven days of life had been in that special care unit before it became clear that switching the machine off was the only kind thing to do. But in that week he'd lived as full a life as he could, and when she first read this story to him his eyes opened and the machines beeped with a much more relaxed rhythm, in spite of his tiny hands that were scrunched up like claws, the parts of him that should have been on the inside but that were instead on the outside wrapped in some sort of protective film, and all those damned wires - so many wires that he looked like the warped invention of an equally warped mad scientist, rather than a baby person. This was the story he needed and every day it had the same effect. A few minutes of calm, of respite.

Now, even all these months later, this story was what *she* needed. She was grieving - she always would be - and reading to him every night, letting him exist in a space he'd never physically been in, simply helped. It shut off the dark and intrusive thoughts for a short while - enough to let her get to sleep and have her body drag her through to the start of another day. Those new days weren't getting any easier yet, but they might do soon. Maybe.

'Alright, mother,' said Jack. 'It's market day today, and I'll soon sell Milky-White, and then we'll see what we can do.'

Bedtime again. Storytime, again. The

same story as every night, of course, and that was absolutely fine - it's the only one that did the trick.

GET MORE TINY TALES...FOR FREE!

Thank you, so much, for reading this collection and making it to the end - I really hope you enjoyed these little stories.

If you did, might I interest you in a few more? And, to sweeten the deal, how about if I give you them for free?

Ok, technically I'm asking for your email address, but that's it. Everyone who signs up to my newsletter gets an exclusive edition of *Tiny Tales of Terror* that isn't available anywhere else. It features the longer story *Mirrored*, then ten more little 'uns to round it out.

If you want to grab your free copy, all you need to do is sign up to my newsletter.

As for the newsletter itself...well, I'm

biased, but I think it's pretty good. Each issue you'll get a short story from me and you'll get a recommendation from me of another indie horror author for you to go and check out. Who knows; they might end up being your new favourite!

Being on the newsletter list is also the easiest way to stay up to date with what I'm doing - be that new releases, giveaways, podcasts, publications…all the good stuff.

And, as I mentioned, you get a whole other volume of *Tiny Tales of Terror* - one that isn't available anywhere else, for free!

So, that link…

davemussonauthor.com/newsletter

ABOUT THE AUTHOR

Dave Musson is a glasses-wearing, bearded human being from the middle of England who likes heavy music with loud guitars, watching movies, and reading creepy stories. He has more hobbies than he should really have time for; playing in a band, hosting a bunch of podcasts, writing, and running a Stephen King-themed YouTube channel.

Dave lives at home with his wife, sons, and annoying dog - he made his debut as a published fiction writer in 2021's *Welcome to the Funhouse*, from Blood Rites. He was also a finalist in the Bellingham Review's 2022 Tobias Wolff Prize for Fiction, and has been published on The Horror Tree, and in *Psychotoxin Press* and *The Reach* Literary magazine.

davemussonauthor.com